TRIGWATER DID IT

LISSA ROVETCH

PUFFIN BOOKS

PUFFIN BOOKS
Published by the Penguin Group
Viking Penguin, a division of Penguin Books USA Inc.,
375 Hudson Street, New York, New York 10014, U.S.A.
Penguin Books Ltd, 27 Wrights Lane, London W8 5TZ, England
Penguin Books Australia Ltd, Ringwood, Victoria, Australia
Penguin Books Canada Ltd, 2801 John Street, Markham, Ontario, Canada L3R 1B4
Penguin Books (N.Z.) Ltd, 182–190 Wairau Road, Auckland 10, New Zealand

Penguin Books Ltd, Registered Offices: Harmondsworth, Middlesex, England

First published in the United States of America by William Morrow and Company, Inc. 1989
Reprinted by arrangement with Greenwillow Books,
a division of William Morrow and Company, Inc.
Published in Picture Puffins, 1991
1   3   5   7   9   10   8   6   4   2
Copyright © Lissa Rovetch, 1989
All rights reserved

LIBRARY OF CONGRESS CATALOGING IN PUBLICATION DATA
Rovetch, Lissa.
Trigwater did it / by Lissa Rovetch.   p.   cm.—(Picture Puffins)
Reprint: Originally published: New York : Morrow, 1989.
Summary: Arnie's invisible friend Trigwater gets him into all
sorts of trouble until Arnie decides to make him behave.
ISBN 0-14-054238-8
[1. Imaginary playmates—Fiction. 2. Behavior—Fiction.]
I. Title.
PZ7.R784Tr   1991   [E]—dc20   90-41417

Printed in Hong Kong

To Kendall,
my husband, my partner, my friend

"French toast with cherries," said Mr. Goodsmile. "My favorite breakfast."

"Mine, too," said Arnie. "I can hardly wait."

"There is plenty for everyone," said Mrs. Goodsmile.

But before you could say lickety-split, the French toast was gone.

"Trigwater did it!" said Arnie. "He ate everything in one bite."

"Really, Arnie," said Mrs. Goodsmile. "You've eaten enough French toast to feed an army, and your poor father must go hungry."

"At least Trigwater left some cherries," said Arnie.

"I don't want to hear another word about that invisible pest," said Mr. Goodsmile. "And no TV for the rest of the day."

Arnie barely made it to the school bus in time. He slid into his favorite seat and checked his lunch box to see what was for dessert.

Just then, Margery Brown turned around and yelled, "Arnie Goodsmile, you pulled my ponytail!"

Arnie looked over at the seat next to him, and there was Trigwater, with a smile on his face. "Trigwater did it," said Arnie. "He pulled your ponytail."

"I don't see anyone," said Margery Brown.

"He's big and green," said Arnie. "And he only lets special people see him."

The school bus stopped, and everyone skipped off.

"You're making up monsters," said Margery Brown. "And I'm going to tell Miss Plumdish."

Arnie and Trigwater rolled their eyes and marched ahead to the classroom.

Class began with the wonders of weather.

"Clouds are remarkable things," said Miss Plumdish. "They're made of millions of tiny water droplets. And what's more..."

But before Miss Plumdish could say another word, a large paper airplane flew by, and it just missed hitting her nose.

"Trigwater did it!" said Arnie. "He is a master airplane flier."

"Is that so?" said Miss Plumdish. "Then let's see how masterful you are at going to the principal's office. Maybe Mr. Muddleberry will know what to do with Trigwater."

Arnie held Trigwater's hand, and they walked bravely down the hall to Mr. Muddleberry's office.

"Well then, Arnie my boy," said Mr. Muddleberry. "What seems to be the problem?"

"It's Trigwater," said Arnie. "Miss Plumdish thinks I'm making him up."

"I see," said Mr. Muddleberry. "You sound like a very unhappy child."

"It's just that Trigwater keeps getting us in trouble," said Arnie.

Mr. Muddleberry paced across the room. "I'm sorry, old sport," he said. "But there's no room for troublemakers at Mapleton Elementary. No sirree Bob, no room at all. You must get rid of your imaginary friend immediately. Or your parents will have to be informed."

Arnie said good-bye to Mr. Muddleberry and held the door open for Trigwater.

After school, Arnie and Trigwater went on a worm hunt. But Arnie's heart wasn't in it. He felt sad and confused. How could he possibly tell Trigwater to leave? Trigwater was a wonderful, magical fellow. He was a nice shade of green, bigger than anyone, and Arnie's best friend in the world.

"There's no other choice," said Arnie. "You must learn to behave, or they'll send you away. Do you think you can do it?"

Trigwater's eyes filled with tears as he nodded his head.

"Good," said Arnie. "Then we'll start right after dinner."

While Trigwater waited for Arnie to have dinner, he drew one last picture on the wall. It was an alligator eating Mr. Muddleberry.

"Now pay attention," Arnie told Trigwater. "This might be our only chance." He dusted off the cover of his mother's old etiquette book and read the first chapter aloud. "From Naughty Pest to Teacher's Pet in Five Easy Steps. Step one," said Arnie. "Always be polite. If you are thoughtful, helpful, and kind, everyone will like to have you around."

Trigwater kept worrying about what would happen if he had to go away. But he listened as hard as he could and tried to remember the rules. Tomorrow would be the test.

The next morning on the school bus, Arnie checked his lunch box to see what was for dessert. "Darn, coconut thinsies again," he said.

"I have a giant piece of magic angel food cake, with confetti sprinkles mixed in," said Margery Brown. "If you take three bites and say the right words, you can fly."

"No one can fly," said Arnie.

"I can," she said. "And I'll prove it at lunch."

Trigwater sat quietly. He could hardly wait to see Margery Brown fly.

It took forever for the lunch bell to ring. At last the clock struck twelve, and Margery Brown led Arnie to the stone bench by the old weeping willow.

She took three bites of cake, climbed up on the bench, and said the magic words, "Angel food cake, raspberry pie, coconut thinsies, and now I can fly."

"Nothing is happening," said Arnie.

Margery Brown flapped her arms and jumped up and down, but she still wasn't flying.

"If you share your cake," said Arnie, "I'll ask Trigwater to give you a boost."

So she gave him the cake and tried one more time. "Angel food cake, raspberry pie, coconut thinsies, and now I can fly."

Margery Brown felt her feet leaving the bench. She went up in the air and felt just like a beautiful bird.

Then, *thump*! She landed on a green bed of grass by the old weeping willow.

The grass felt soft and warm. It held her with its long grassy arms, it tickled her with its smooth grassy fingers, and it comforted her with a grassy-green smile.

Margery Brown rubbed the stars from her eyes. "Hello, Trigwater," she said. "I'm very pleased to meet you."

After lunch, the class continued their weather studies. Arnie drew the most beautiful picture of a cumulus cloud Miss Plumdish had ever seen. And Trigwater didn't fly a single airplane.

"I am delighted with your excellent behavior," said Miss Plumdish. "It is hard to believe this is the same Arnie Goodsmile who caused such a commotion just the other day."

Margery Brown went home with Arnie to watch their favorite cartoons.

"Did you have a good day?" asked Mrs. Goodsmile.

"I flew at lunch," exclaimed Margery Brown. "And I landed in Trigwater's arms!"

"Trigwater's arms?" said Mrs. Goodsmile. "You mean you've seen Trigwater, too?"

Arnie changed the subject by handing his mother a crumpled-up note from Miss Plumdish. It said:

Dear Mr. and Mrs. Goodsmile,
Arnie's classroom conduct has improved so much that I wanted to send this gold star of excellence home with him.
Sincerely yours,
Alma Jean Plumdish

Mrs. Goodsmile gave Arnie a big hug and invited Margery Brown to stay for dinner.

There was rainbow trout with corn on the cob, and banana splits for dessert.

"Miss Plumdish is right, Arnie," said Mrs. Goodsmile. "You *have* been a perfect little lamb lately."

"And don't forget Trigwater." Mr. Goodsmile laughed. "He didn't steal any of my strudel this morning and he hasn't touched our dinner tonight."

"That's right," said Mrs. Goodsmile. "Poor Trigwater must be starving by now."

"Don't worry," said Arnie. "I think Trigwater can take care of himself."